SO-AEX-447

DETECTIVE MOLE

written and illustrated by
ROBERT QUACKENBUSH

★

Lothrop, Lee & Shepard Company
A Division of William Morrow & Company, Inc.

NEW YORK

MANHASSET PUBLIC LIBRARY

[BEGINNING
READER]
Quackenbush

Also by Robert Quackenbush
ANIMAL CRACKS

For Piet's sake!

Copyright © 1976 by Robert Quackenbush.

All rights reserved. No part of this book may be reproduced or utilized in any form or by any means, electronic or mechanical, including photocopying, recording or by any information retrieval system, without permission in writing from the Publisher. Inquiries should be addressed to Lothrop, Lee and Shepard Company, 105 Madison Ave., New York, N.Y. 10016.

Printed in the United States of America.

1 2 3 4 5 80 79 78 77 76

Library of Congress Cataloging in Publication Data

Quackenbush, Robert M
    Detective Mole.

   SUMMARY: Detective Mole finds solutions to other animals' mysteries in five easy-to-read stories.
    [1. Moles (Animals)—Fiction.   2. Mystery and detective stories]   I. Title.
PZ7.Q16De   [Fic]   75-25806
ISBN 0-688-41726-4
ISBN 0-688-51726-9 lib. bdg.

CONTENTS

1

THE CASE OF THE
GHOST IN THE CHICKEN COOP

When Maynard Mole finished
detective school,
he dug himself a fine office.
Then he hung up a sign:

DETECTIVE MOLE
PRIVATE EYE

Word got around that there
was a detective in town.
Early one morning the phone rang.
It was Mrs. Hen.

"Help! Help!" she cried.

"There's a ghost in our coop.

Come at once!"

Detective Mole grabbed his

magnifying glass and ran

to Chicken Coop 5.

He knocked on the chimney.

Mr. Rooster opened the door.

"The door is over here," he said.

"Sorry about that," Detective Mole

said. "It's very bright out here."

He put his sunglasses away and

went inside.

He asked Mr. Rooster and Mrs. Hen

to tell him about the ghost.

"For three nights we have heard
a spooky voice in the attic,"
said Mr. Rooster. "But when
I go up to look, no one is there.
It must be a ghost!"
Detective Mole asked what the
spooky voice said.
"The first night we thought it said,
DO NOT FEED YOUR CHILDREN
SPINACH," said Mr. Rooster.
"The second night we thought it said,
DO NOT SEND YOUR CHILDREN
TO SCHOOL.
But last night we were sure it said,
THIS IS YOUR LAST WARNING.

DO NOT FEED YOUR CHILDREN
SPINACH.
DO NOT SEND YOUR CHILDREN
TO SCHOOL."

"It was horrible," Mrs. Hen sobbed.
"The ghost keeps talking about
our chicks. I'm sure they are
in danger!"

Detective Mole asked if the chicks
knew anything about the ghost.
Mrs. Hen said that she hadn't
told them about it.
"I thought they would be too
frightened!" she said.
"I'm sure the chicks didn't hear
the ghost," Mr. Rooster said.
"I looked in to make sure
they were all right. They
were all safely in their beds."
"They are at school now,"
said Mrs. Hen. "But we were
almost afraid to send them
this morning."

"Hmmm," said Detective Mole.

He went into the chicks' bedroom.

He looked carefully at everything
in the room.

He even looked out the window.

Then he took his detective manual
from his pocket.
He looked up the famous
BROKEN RAIN PIPE MYSTERY.
"I thought this case had a
familiar ring to it," he said.
"I want to hear this ghost
tonight for myself."
He asked where he could hide without
letting the chicks know.
"What about the clothes hamper?"
asked Mrs. Hen.
"The very place," said Detective
Mole.

That night Detective Mole was
squashed in the crowded hamper,
waiting for the ghost.

Mr. Rooster leaned over the hamper.
"If you find my gold tie pin
while you're in there," he
whispered, "please hold on to it.
I've been looking for it
everywhere."

Then Mr. Rooster went to bed.
Just after the clock struck midnight,
Detective Mole heard a loud,
moaning voice.

"THIS IS YOUR VERY LAST
WARNING.

DO NOT FEED YOUR CHILDREN
SPINACH.
DO NOT SEND YOUR CHILDREN
TO SCHOOL!"

Detective Mole climbed carefully
out of the clothes hamper.

He tiptoed to the door
of the chicks' room.
He opened the door very quietly.
Then Mr. Rooster and Mrs. Hen
heard a loud cheeping noise.
They ran to the chicks' room.

Detective Mole was holding the chicks
by the collars of their nightshirts.
"Aha!" he said. "Here is your ghost,
caught red-handed!"
"Goodness gracious!" Mrs. Hen said.
"How can that be?"
Detective Mole told her how
he had solved the mystery.
"I noticed the rain pipe outside
the chicks' bedroom," he said.
"There is a hole in it next to
their window. I figured that if
the chicks spoke through the hole,
their voices would echo in the
attic."

"Think of that!" said Mr. Rooster.

"You naughty chicks!" said Mrs. Hen.

"What a scare you gave us!"

"Back to bed now," Mr. Rooster

said. "You must get up early

to go to school."

"Phooey!" said the chicks.

"We didn't know you had called
a detective!"

"I'm glad the ghost mystery is
solved," Mr. Rooster said. "But
I wish you could solve the mystery
of my missing tie pin."

Detective Mole thumbed through
his detective manual.

"My manual says that may be
a ghost of another color," he said.
"I'll check it out."

2 THE CASE OF THE MISSING TOE SHOES

The next phone call came from
Miss Field Mouse.
She asked Detective Mole to come
at once to Mrs. Rabbit's house.
He grabbed his magnifying glass
and ran to the house.
Mrs. Rabbit led him into the
living room.
"Detective Mole at your service,"
he said, talking to a footstool.

"I'm over here," Miss Field Mouse
said from a nearby chair.
"Sorry about that," said Detective
Mole. "I forgot to take off
my sunglasses."

He asked Miss Field Mouse
why she had called.
"My toe shoes are missing!" she said.
"I must find them. I am going
to dance at Town Hall tonight.
It will be my very first time
on a real stage!"
"When did you notice that
your toe shoes were missing?"
Detective Mole asked.
Miss Field Mouse said she had come
to babysit at Mrs. Rabbit's house
the night before.
She had brought her toe shoes
with her.

"I planned to practice my twirls
and spins after I put the bunnies
to bed," she said. "But when
I looked in my bag for my toe shoes,
they were gone!"

Mrs. Rabbit patted Miss Field Mouse's
paw.

"When we got home, we searched
the house," said Mrs. Rabbit.

"We couldn't find the toe shoes
anywhere. We searched again today.
They are nowhere to be found!"

Miss Field Mouse said she believed
that someone had stolen her toe
shoes.

"Someone must be jealous
of my chance to perform
at Town Hall," she sobbed.
"I practiced for years for this
moment. I paid for my own lessons
with my babysitting money.
Now all is lost!"

Detective Mole asked Mrs. Rabbit
if he could speak to her bunnies
about the missing toe shoes.
Mrs. Rabbit said that her bunnies
were too little to talk.
They were both still teething.
"Teething, you say?" said Detective
Mole. "That brings to mind a famous
case in my detective manual—
THE TEETHING TIGER MYSTERY.
May I take a look at the
bunnies' crib?"
Mrs. Rabbit led him into the bedroom.
Detective Mole pulled out his
magnifying glass.
He began to search.

Suddenly he pulled the toe shoes
out from under a pillow.

"Aha!" said Detective Mole.

"Oh, dear," Mrs. Rabbit said.

"My bunnies have been using
the toe shoes for teething.

How did they ever get them?"

"We may never know," answered
Detective Mole.
He took the toe shoes
to Miss Field Mouse.
She was thrilled to see them
again.
"But some of the rhinestones
are missing," she said. "Do you
think they fell off somewhere?"
Detective Mole thumbed through
his detective manual.
"My manual says to leave no
stone unturned," he said.
"I'll check it out."

3 THE CASE OF THE
TERRIBLE WATER TORTURE

Mr. and Mrs. Cat called
Detective Mole.
They said they needed help.
Detective Mole grabbed his
magnifying glass and ran to
their basement apartment.
This time he remembered to take off
his sunglasses when he went in.
"Detective Mole at your service,"
he said to Mr. and Mrs. Cat.

"Thank goodness you're here,"
Mr. Cat said. "I am sure we are
the victims of a dreadful plot.
An evil gang of spies must be after us.
We are being tortured in our
very home by a person or persons
unknown and unseen."
"How do you mean?" asked Detective
Mole.
Mr. Cat said they had been getting
messages in code in the mail.
And every night they were awakened
by a horrid drip, drip of water
on their foreheads.

"You know how we cats hate water,"
Mr. Cat said.
"Who could be doing this to us?"
asked Mrs. Cat.

Then she said she had also
noticed that some tinsel from
their year-round Christmas tree
had disappeared.

"You just imagine that,"
Mr. Cat said to her.
"I keep telling you that spies
would not be interested in tinsel."

"Where does the water torture
happen?" asked Detective Mole.
"In here," Mr. Cat said,
opening the bedroom door.
Detective Mole looked all around.
He looked up at the ceiling.

Then he took his detective manual
from his pocket.
He turned to the famous
DRIPPING WATER HOSE MYSTERY.
"I thought this case sounded
familiar," he said.

He asked for a chair to stand on.
Then he looked carefully at each
pipe.

"Aha!" he said after a few moments.
"Here is the cause of your water
torture. A leaky pipe."

Mr. and Mrs. Cat looked amazed.

But then Mr. Cat held up the

coded messages.

"How do you explain these?" he asked.

"Look at this one that came today.

It says, THIS IS YOUR

FINAL NOTICE.

And look at all those numbers.

I'm sure it is a secret code."

Detective Mole looked at the messages.

"Have you paid your water

bill lately?" he asked.

"Water bill?" Mr. Cat said.

"What does that have to do

with a gang of spies?"

"These messages are from the Water Company," Detective Mole replied. "They are asking you to pay your bill."

"How embarrassing," Mr. Cat said. "But we won't pay the bill until that leaky pipe is fixed."

"What about my missing Christmas tree tinsel?" Mrs. Cat asked.

Detective Mole opened his detective manual again.

"My manual says not to judge a tree by its bark," he said. "I'll check it out."

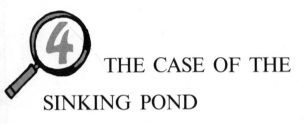 THE CASE OF THE

SINKING POND

Detective Mole got a call from
Mrs. Duck.
He grabbed his magnifying glass
and ran to the pond.
"Detective Mole at your service,"
he said.
He was talking to a water lily.
Mrs. Duck swam toward him.
"Here I am," she said.
"Sorry about that," Detective Mole
said. "My sunglasses were fogged."

He asked Mrs. Duck to tell him
her problem.

"My pond is slowly sinking,"
she said. "My feet drag
on the bottom as I swim.
I'm sure someone is stealing
the water. If this keeps up,
my poor ducklings will never
learn their water tricks."

Detective Mole took his detective
manual from his pocket.

"This reminds me of the famous
DISAPPEARING MINERAL
WATER MYSTERY," he said.

He searched the edge of the pond
with his magnifying glass.
He found some hoof prints.
They went across Mrs. Duck's
back yard and out the gate.
"Aha!" he said. "I think I have
solved this case."

Mrs. Duck and her ducklings
followed the trail of hoof prints
with Detective Mole.
The prints led them to Mr. and
Mrs. Horse's back yard.
Mrs. Horse was pouring a bucket
of pond water into some empty
bottles.
Detective Mole quietly slipped
up behind her.
"Caught in the act!" he said.
Mrs. Horse jumped in surprise.
She dropped the bucket and
the bottles.

Mrs. Duck was very angry.
"Why are you taking the water
from my pond?" she demanded.
Mrs. Horse explained that she
didn't think Mrs. Duck would mind.
"The pond water has such
good minerals," she said.
"And Mr. Horse has been drinking
too much root beer. So I am
filling his empty root beer
bottles with your good water.
I want my husband to drink
mineral water instead of
root beer. It is so much
better for him."

"Humph!" said Mrs. Duck.

"Your idea is not better for me.

My pond is sinking!"

Mrs. Horse said, "Dear me.

I didn't know that. Please

forgive me."

They had always been good friends,
so Mrs. Duck forgave her.
"Besides, it will rain soon,"
she said. "The pond will fill up again."

"I couldn't bottle much more
of the water anyway," Mrs. Horse
said. "Almost all of my metal
bottle caps have disappeared.
It is a real mystery. I can't
imagine what happened to them."
Detective Mole thumbed through
his detective manual.
"My manual says there is
something about this that
doesn't hold water," he said.
"I'll check it out."

5 THE CASE OF THE LONESOME STRANGER

Detective Mole went to his office
early the next day.

His phone rang all morning.

Mr. Rooster said he still hadn't
found his gold tie pin.

Miss Field Mouse said *all* the
rhinestones were gone from her
toe shoes.

It had happened after her smash
hit at Town Hall.

Mrs. Cat said that every bit of
tinsel had disappeared from her
year-round Christmas tree.
Mrs. Horse said that all her
bottle caps were gone.
Other animals also called
to report missing shiny objects.
Everyone was sure there was
a thief in town.
Detective Mole asked them all
to come to his office.
"I've asked you to meet here,"
he said, "because I believe
you are all part of the same case.

Each of you has lost something
shiny. The question is,
who would want these things?"

He took out his detective manual.
"This case sounds like the famous
MISSING TIN FOIL MYSTERY,"
he said. "Has anyone new
moved into town?"
Elmo Elephant said that a
Mr. Pack Rat had moved in

next door to him.

He was a lonesome stranger from

the desert way out west.

"I think I'll pay Mr. Pack Rat

a visit," Detective Mole said.

Everyone raced down the street

with him.

Mr. Pack Rat greeted them
at his door.
He looked surprised.
"How nice of you to come
and visit," he said. "I was
just about to invite you all
to my get-acquainted party.
Do come in."
Everyone marched inside.
When they looked around,
they all gasped.
The house was decorated with
all their shiny things!

"Doesn't it look nice?" asked
Mr. Pack Rat. "I borrowed
such beautiful things."
"BORROWED?" everyone
shouted at once.
"Why, yes," said Mr. Pack Rat.
"I had to borrow them. My own
things have not arrived yet from
out west. I needed decorations
for my get-acquainted party.
We pack rats can't stand a house
without any shiny things. It
just doesn't seem like home."
Detective Mole turned to the
angry crowd.

"Let me explain," he said.

He told them that pack rats always
borrowed shiny things from each
other.

They looked for other shiny objects
to make their desert homes look
nice.

"The famous case of the missing
tin foil gave me the clue,"
he said.
Mr. Pack Rat said that he was
very sorry he had borrowed things
without asking.

He had planned to return everything
after the party.

"Look at it this way," he said.

"I'm very good at finding things.
You can come to me whenever you
lose something. I'll be able
to find it for you."

Detective Mole was worried.

He thought Mr. Pack Rat might

take business away from him.

So he hired Mr. Pack Rat as his

partner on the spot.

Everyone stayed for the party
and had a wonderful time.
Mr. Pack Rat returned their
shiny things.
They were all very happy.
Happy, that is, until Detective
Mole handed each of them a bill.
When they complained,
Detective Mole took out
his detective manual.
"My manual says that
when a case is solved,
one good turn deserves
another," he said.
"I don't have to check that out."